A NORTH-SOUTH PAPERBACK

Critical praise for

Mia the Beach Cat

"This is a light breeze of an early-reader book, coaching new readers' skills with a story close enough to real life to be comfortable, but spiked with sufficient suspense to be interesting. The format is clean and open, and amiable, unbabyish pencil-and-watercolor illustrations appear on every page, giving plenty of clues to the text."

Bulletin of the Center for Children's Books

"The writing is simple, and the book is filled with enough detail and dialogue to hold young readers' attention. The warm, muted watercolors are filled with action. An easy-to-read story for children ready for more than one sentence per page." *School Library Journal*

"An appealing story for young animal lovers." *Kirkus*

"Both the story and the artwork . . . are engaging."

The Horn Book Guide

MIA
THE BEACH CAT

A STORY BY

Wolfram Hänel

ILLUSTRATED BY

Kirsten Höcker

TRANSLATED BY

J. Alison James

North-South Books
New York   London

Copyright © 1994 by Nord-Süd Verlag AG, Gossau Zürich, Switzerland
First published in Switzerland under the title *Mia die Strandkatze*
English translation copyright © 1994 by North-South Books, Inc.

First published in the United States, Great Britain, Canada,
Australia, and New Zealand in 1994 by North-South Books,
an imprint of Nord-Süd Verlag AG, Gossau Zürich, Switzerland.
First paperback edition published in 1995

Distributed in the United States by North-South Books Inc., New York.

Library of Congress Cataloging-in-Publication Data.
Hänel, Wolfram.
[Mia die Strandkatze. English]
Mia the beach cat: a story/ by Wolfram Hänel;
illustrated by Kirsten Höcker; translated by J. Alison James
Summary: While vacationing at the beach with her parents,
Maggie becomes inseparable with a little cat she finds
playing in the waves.
[1. Beaches—Fiction. 2. Cats—Fiction. 3. Friendship—Fiction.]
I. James, J. Alison. II. Höcker, Kirstin, ill. III. Title.
PZ7.H1928Mi 1994
[E]—dc20   94-5064
ISBN 1-55858-314-9 (TRADE BINDING)
1 3 5 7 9 TB 10 8 6 4 2
ISBN 1-55858-315-7 (LIBRARY BINDING)
3 5 7 9 LB 10 8 6 4 2
ISBN 1-55858-508-7 (PAPERBACK)
3 5 7 9 PB 10 8 6 4 2

A CIP catalogue record for this book is available
from The British Library.
Printed in Belgium

One sunny holiday, Maggie went to the sea.

Of course, she didn't go alone.

She went with her mother and her father and Felix, her stuffed tiger.

But Felix wasn't much fun at the beach. He kept getting sand in his fur.

And she couldn't take him swimming. If he got wet, his stuffing would get all lumpy.

Maggie's parents weren't much fun either. Maggie's mother lay on her beach chair all day long. Maggie's father lay on his beach chair beside her. All day long. They said things like, "Ahh, isn't this wonderful!" They never even opened their eyes. Except when they couldn't find the suntan lotion.

Maggie's parents did not even swim.
Mother said the waves were *much* too high. Father nodded and said that the water was *much* too cold.

Then he pulled his straw hat down over his face and went back to sleep.

At first Maggie did not mind. She built a sand castle. Then another one. She even dug a moat with a canal that went right down to the sea and filled up with water. That was a lot of work!

Then Maggie collected shells—mussel shells and oyster shells and conch shells. Conch shells were the best, though they were hard to find. When Maggie held one up to her ear, she could hear the roaring of all the oceans in the world!

Of course Maggie collected stones. Flat ones and round ones and even a stone with a hole through the middle. She found polished sea glass and feathers and crab claws. She found a nice piece of wood and an old rope, some green and purple seaweed and a torn fishing net.

But what good is a collection if you have no one to share it with?

Sadly Maggie sat at the water's edge and stared at the waves. She stretched out her toes and wondered if the next wave would wash up and touch them.

A fat sea gull stood near Maggie. Suddenly the gull flapped away, screeching loudly.

That's funny, thought Maggie. What's frightened the bird?

Then Maggie saw it. A little grey and white cat playing with the waves! So that was why the gull flew away.

The little cat crept close to the breakers. Then, just when a wave came, it dashed back to the safe dry sand.

Another wave rumbled in like thunder.
It was as huge as a car. With a flying
leap, the cat escaped the wave and
landed right at Maggie's feet.

Maggie clapped her hands and cried,
"That was wonderful!"

The cat blinked and went "Mia..."
It didn't say "Meow," like regular cats do.
Just "Mia."

Now this is something, Maggie thought. A cat who plays tag with the waves and who only says "Mia."

"I know," Maggie cried. "I'll call you Mia. That is a good name for a cat. Maggie and Mia. They sound good together, don't you think?"

The cat yawned. It stretched and rubbed its back against Maggie's legs.

Then it took off for the water. When the next wave broke, it scampered back. Then down to the water's edge again, and back to the sand. Down to the edge and back, again and again.

Now and then it would blink at Maggie and say "Mia!" until Maggie understood what it was trying to tell her: Come and play with me!

But Maggie's parents had already
packed up their chairs. Maggie's father
called, "It's time to go, Maggie."

"Will you be here tomorrow?" Maggie
asked the little cat.

Mia blinked and said, "Mia!"

As Maggie trudged up the dunes
behind her parents, the little cat
followed.

Maggie's father had barely opened the
door to the car when Mia jumped onto
the back seat.

"Help! A stray cat!" shrieked Maggie's mother, and her father picked it up by the scruff of its neck and said, "Out you go."

"But that's *my* cat," Maggie said. "We've been playing in the waves all afternoon. She's my friend. Her name is Mia. That's because she doesn't say meow, she only says—"

"Mia!" said Mia.

"See what I mean?" Maggie said proudly.

"No cats in my car," said Maggie's mother. "And that's final."

"But we can't just leave her here!" said Maggie.

But her father had already started the car and was pulling away. And Mia stayed behind, all alone on the dunes.

The next morning Maggie ate her breakfast in no time at all. At last they were on their way to the beach again. And guess who was sitting there on the big sand dune, blinking? It was Mia! She looked as if she had spent the entire night waiting right there for Maggie.

Maggie burst out of the car and ran
after Mia, over the big dune, across the
beach, down to the water.

And there they played with the waves.
They dashed to the water's edge and
jumped back, down and back, down and
back they went.

When they were tired, they lay in the sun and snuggled each other. Maggie stroked Mia's fur. Mia squeezed her eyes shut and purred like an old fan.

In the evening Mia followed Maggie
as far as the car.

And the next morning the little cat
was there, waiting on the dunes.

That day Maggie brought along her stuffed tiger, Felix. She had a silly idea. She put Felix on a long leash and sat him at the water's edge.

As soon as a wave started to break, she
yanked him back up to the dry sand.

It was great fun until…

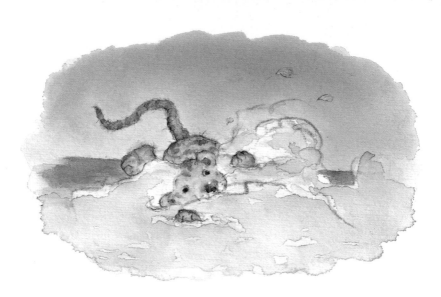

Felix got stuck on a rock, and the wave crashed over him. He slipped right out of his leash, and the wave washed him out to sea!

Maggie and Mia watched helplessly. Now and then they caught a glimpse of a few tiger stripes between the waves. Then Felix disappeared completely.

"It doesn't matter," Maggie said loudly.
She scratched Mia behind her ears. "Now
I have you. When you have a real cat,
who needs a stuffed one?" She sighed.
"If only I could take you home."

Mia blinked and said, "Mia…"

The next morning Mia was nowhere to be seen.

Maggie knew the little cat was just hiding somewhere, playing a game. She searched in the dune grass. She looked under an old boat, and behind the little beach house where the toilets were.

But there was no sign of Mia. Nothing! What if something had happened to her?

Maggie thought of how the waves had washed away Felix! Mia was so small, and Maggie was sure she couldn't swim!

Frantic with worry, Maggie ran to her father.

"Come now," he said. "Your little cat knows how to look out for herself. I'm sure nothing has happened to her. I expect we'll find her waiting for you tomorrow morning."

But the next morning Mia was still missing. Maggie sat on the big sand dune and cried.

After a little while she started to think things over, like a detective.

If only she knew where Mia slept, thought Maggie. Maybe in an old rubber boot, or an overturned fishing crate.

Fishing crate. That's it—fish! All cats like fish. And the sea was filled with fish. And where are fish brought in from the sea?

Maggie ran excitedly to her father and cried, "Daddy! Daddy! I think I know where Mia is! She probably got hungry and went down to the fishing boats to find something to eat!"

Groaning, Maggie's father pulled on his clothes and went up to the car.

But there was not a single fishing boat at the docks. And no sign at all of Mia. Only an old man looking out to sea.

"Excuse me," said Maggie. "Did you see a cat? A little cat that goes 'Mia'?"

"Hmm now. I'll just have to think about that." He scratched his head, pushing back his cap. Then he shook his head sadly. "Nope," he said. "Can't say that I have."

Then suddenly he sat up. "Wait one minute!" he said, his eyes squinting. "There was a little cat. There was. Scuttling round here with its nose to the ground and its tail in the air. That was—let me see—it was right before the boats went out this morning. I'll just bet you she jumped aboard and is sailing the seas this very minute."

"Did you hear that, Daddy!" Maggie cried. "Mia is on a fishing boat!"

"When do the boats come back in?" Maggie's father asked the old man.

"It can't be too much longer," he answered.

And just then, right on the edge of the horizon, the first fishing boat sailed into view.

"Do you have my cat on board?" Maggie asked before the fisherman had even had a chance to dock.

"Nope," said the fisherman. "Can't say that I have. Just a fine catch of cod and flounder and a few fat crabs. But no cats!"

"Then Mia must be on the next boat," Maggie said, and again she looked anxiously out to sea.

By then Maggie's father was just as worried as she was. He watched the horizon and paced back and forth along the dock.

Finally the next fishing boat arrived.
But no sign of Mia.

Maggie's shoulders drooped in despair.

"Come now," Maggie's father said, and
he patted her on the head.

Suddenly he called: "Look there!
Another boat is coming!"

And soon Maggie cried, "There she is!
See her? In the front!"

And there she was. Perched high on
the prow, Mia stood blinking. Maggie
could almost hear her say "Mia!"

Then suddenly the little cat saw
Maggie. With a gigantic leap she tried to
jump across the water into Maggie's arms.
But the boat was still too far away!

Splash! Mia plunged into the dirty water! Desperately she paddled for her life.

"Cat overboard! Engines in reverse!" cried the fisherman.

Maggie's father grabbed a life preserver and threw it into the water. It worked! Mia fastened her claws on the ring.

Quickly the fisherman took a long boat hook and fished out the cat.

The fisherman jumped ashore and pressed the sopping wet Mia into Maggie's arms.

"Here you are," he said kindly. "You can have your little stowaway back. She polished off two whole cod. Only left the bones, licked clean."

Happily Maggie climbed back into the car. Maggie's father turned around from the front seat and scratched Mia under the chin. Mia purred like an old fan and said "Mia."

The next few days seemed to fly past. Maggie and Mia played from morning till night on the beach. The game they liked best was chasing waves—in and out, in and out. Once, Maggie's father played, but he was not fast enough, and he got splashed by the first wave.

Then it was their last day. Maggie's parents packed their suitcases. Maggie watched, quietly stroking Mia. She was trying to think of a way to smuggle Mia into the car. Finally she had an idea...

Maggie's mother was driving. Maggie's
father read the map.

Maggie secretly stuck her finger into
the basket and rubbed Mia's moist nose.

"I wonder where the little cat is, now that you're gone?" Maggie's mother said.

"Hmmm," Maggie said. "I wonder."

Then the traffic got heavier, and Maggie's mother didn't have time to think about the cat anymore.

But Maggie's father turned around in his seat...

Carefully, quietly, he slipped his hand into the basket; he winked at Maggie. And they heard a soft fluttering sound, like an old fan. Mia was purring.

About the Illustrator

KIRSTEN HÖCKER was born in a small town near Osnabrück, Germany. She began studying art history, then went into illustration at the Berlin School of Fine Arts. Since graduating, she has created illustrations for picture books, children's television shows, newspapers, and book jackets.

Kirsten Höcker lives and works in Berlin and in Metz, France. Because she grew up on a farm, she is partial to stories that feature animals, and girls like Maggie.

About the Author

WOLFRAM HÄNEL has lived for most of his life in Hannover, Germany. He studied German and English literature and has worked as a photographer, a graphic artist, a copy writer, a teacher, and a playwright. Today Wolfram Hänel writes children's books, plays, and travel guides.

Wolfram Hänel loves lighthouses and fishing boats and islands with long beaches—and of course his wife and daughter. His best friends live in Ireland, and it was there that he experienced this story firsthand.

Other North-South Paperback Easy-to-Read Books